Budgie

At Bendick's Point

Read it Again
3630 Peachtree Pkwy., Ste 314
Suwanee, GA 30024
770-232-9331
www.Read-it-Again.com

D1410616

For Andrew

First Aladdin Paperbacks edition April 1996
Text © 1989 by H.R.H. The Duchess of York
Illustrations © 1989 by Simon & Schuster, Inc.

Aladdin Paperbacks
An imprint of Simon & Schuster
Children's Publishing Division
1230 Avenue of the Americas
New York, NY 10020

All rights reserved, including the right of
reproduction in whole or in part in any form

Also available in a Simon & Schuster Books for Young Readers edition

The text of this book was set in 16-point Stempel Schneidler.

Printed and bound in the United States of America

10 9 8 7 6 5 4 3 2 1

ISBN 0-689-80849-6

Budgie

At Bendick's Point

H.R.H. The Duchess of York
Illustrated by John Richardson

Aladdin Paperbacks

Dring, dring went the alarm. At last the day of the air show had arrived. Everyone in the hangar was excited. Everyone, that is, except for Budgie, the little helicopter.

"Not much point in **my** getting up," he thought. "I'm going back to sleep."

But Budgie couldn't get back to sleep. Every time he closed his eyes he saw flocks of sheep. Budgie knew it was naughty to chase animals, but when he was out last week he hadn't been able to stop himself. He had hoped no one would see him. Why did Lionel have to fly by just then?

So now Lionel insisted that Budgie do the parcel deliveries
on the day of the air show. Budgie watched Lionel
polish his medals and then begin inspecting the planes
and helicopters as they came out of the helicopter wash.
"There goes scruffy Budgie," said Lionel as Budgie passed.

"I'm glad he's not in the air show, especially my surprise
  demonstration."
"I don't mind missing the inspection and clean-up one bit,"
  said Budgie, as he rose into the air.
"Bye-bye, Budgie," shouted Pippa after him.

As he flew along the coast towards Bendick's Point, Budgie cheered
up. The sea was sparkling and the cold wind whipped his cheeks.
He almost forgot about the air show and what he was missing.

As he looked down, he saw two boys preparing to go out for the day in their boat. They waved to Budgie as he passed.

As usual, Captain Frobisher was waiting for Budgie when he arrived
at the lighthouse at Bendick's Point.
"Be careful!" shouted the Captain as Budgie lowered the rope. "There's
a gale warning and the wind is getting stronger every minute."
It was difficult to hover, but after two or three tries Budgie managed
to unload his parcels.
"I'd better get on with my deliveries," thought Budgie, "before the
wind gets any worse. They'll be starting the air show about now.
I wonder how it's going."

When Budgie returned, the air show was well underway. But watching the display made him feel left out. "I know," he thought, "I'll listen to my radio. *Helicopter Heroes*, my favorite program, is on." Just then, Budgie's emergency channel came to life. "*Mayday, mayday. Mayday, mayday.*"

"Hold on," said Budgie. "That sounds like Captain Frobisher."

Budgie listened hard. The message **was** from Bendick's Point. The two boys were in trouble. "Quick," said Budgie. "I'd better raise the alarm. I **do** wish Pippa was here."

But as he hopped towards the siren, Budgie realized that no one would hear him. The air show was at its exciting climax with Lionel's surprise demonstration. Lionel and Chin-up, the Chinook, were lifting huge weights on a metal cable. It was breathtaking to watch. Budgie tried to attract their attention but, just then, there was a loud crack.

The cable had snapped! It whipped up and hit Lionel's rotors, knocking him into a spin.

"Oh no," shouted Budgie.

At that moment, Pippa appeared.

The two friends gasped as Lionel made his emergency landing. His rotors were completely bent. The fire engines quickly approached. But Budgie hadn't forgotten

the distress call. He quickly explained to Pippa what had happened. "Come on," he said. "We haven't much time. We'd better go on our own."

Soon Budgie and Pippa saw the familiar rocky coast and Bendick's Point. The gale was getting worse so Pippa circled high above the storm to keep radio contact with the lighthouse. Budgie flew out to sea and then approached the cliffs. He couldn't see much because

the rain beat so heavily into his eyes. At last he caught sight of the
little boat. The boys were trapped in a narrow cove and the tide
was rising. Never had Budgie seen rocks so sharp.
"Good luck, Budgie," radioed Pippa.

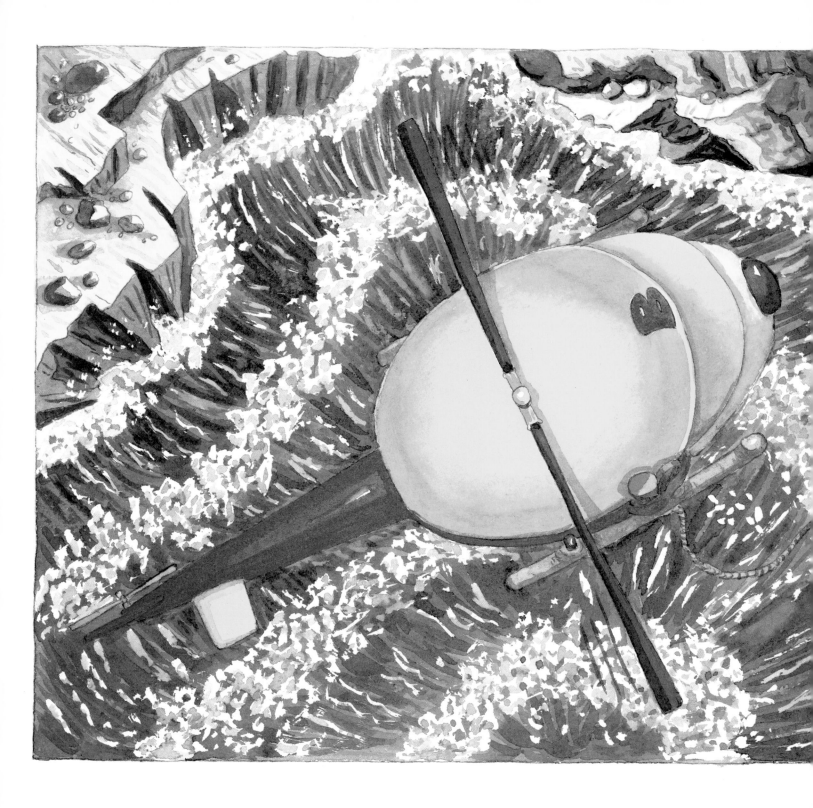

"Help, help!" Budgie heard the boys cry.
"I'd better lower a rope," thought Budgie. "It's our only hope in this rough sea." "Hold on!" he shouted to the boys, but they couldn't hear.

The wind was too strong. All at once a huge, roaring wave hit Budgie's skids and knocked him off balance. Budgie let go of the rope and swerved upwards.

The storm was getting worse. "I wish I was back at the hangar," thought Budgie. He looked at Pippa circling above. Budgie knew that a helicopter was stronger in this weather than a small plane. "It's all up to me," he thought. He held his breath as he swooped again into the cove. He hovered for a moment and shouted, "Quick, hang on tight, boys! We're going up."

Using **all** his strength, Budgie rose to the
top of the cliff. Just as he reached safety,
the boys let go of the skids. People rushed
towards them.

"Thanks, Budgie," they shouted.
"It's too dangerous to land here, Pippa," said Budgie.
"Let's go back home before the weather
  gets worse."

On the way back to the hangar, Pippa radioed ahead to
tell everyone about Budgie's brave rescue. When the two
friends arrived there was a loud cheer. Lionel blushed as
he limped forward. "Er… hurumph," he cleared his throat.

"Budgie, you and Pippa have both been very brave." As he spoke, Lionel presented Budgie with a gleaming medal. Budgie beamed.

"And now," said Lionel, "we've got a surprise for you."

Budgie had never felt happier than when he led the flypast.

What an exciting end to an exciting day.